Taylor
the Talent Show Fairy

Special thanks to
Sue Mongredien

ORCHARD BOOKS
338 Euston Road, London NW1 3BH
Orchard Books Australia
Level 17/207 Kent Street, Sydney, NSW 2000

A Paperback Original
First published in 2011 by Orchard Books

HiT entertainment

Illustrations © Orchard Books 2011

A CIP catalogue record for this book is available
from the British Library.

ISBN 978 1 40831 290 2

3 5 7 9 10 8 6 4 2

Printed in Great Britain

The paper and board used in this paperback are natural recyclable
products made from wood grown in sustainable forests. The
manufacturing processes conform to the environmental regulations
of the country of origin.

Orchard Books is a division of Hachette Children's Books,
an Hachette UK company.

www.hachette.co.uk

Taylor
the Talent Show
Fairy

by Daisy Meadows

ORCHARD BOOKS

www.rainbowmagic.co.uk

Who likes talent shows? Not me!
So, goblins, listen carefully,
Each Showtime Fairy has a star,
Their magic glitters near and far.

Now do exactly as I say,
And steal these magical stars away,
Then, when our wicked work is done,
We can spoil all showtime fun!

Contents

Flying the Flag

"Wow!" said Kirsty Tate, as she walked into the Cooke football stadium. Music boomed out, and there were people everywhere, queuing for souvenirs, chatting to friends and filing in to their seats. "It's buzzing in here!"

Her best friend, Rachel Walker, grinned at her, feeling excited. "It's the perfect place to spend our last night together."

Kirsty had been staying with Rachel for half term, and they'd come out this evening with Rachel's parents to watch the Tippington Variety Show, which was being held to raise funds for a nearby park. There was a large stage in the centre of the stadium, decorated with golden stars that glittered in the spotlights. The audience were dressed in different colours, according to which school they supported.

Some wore green, some wore red, and some were in blue and gold, the colours of Rachel's school – Tippington School. Kirsty and Rachel both wore blue hooded tops and jeans, and had painted blue and gold stars on their faces.

"This is going to be brilliant," Rachel said happily. Then she frowned. "Well… if Jack Frost doesn't ruin it, of course," she muttered under her breath.

Kirsty nodded, glancing around apprehensively. All week, she and Rachel had been cheering on the students of Tippington School as they competed in different heats.

There had been magicians, actors, acrobats, dancers, singers and ice skaters – and tonight, the best performers from each event were joining together in the Variety Show. It had been a wonderful week – and a very magical one, too!

Kirsty and Rachel had enjoyed some amazing adventures with their new friends, the Showtime Fairies, as they helped them find their missing magic stars.

The only problem was that mean Jack Frost had tried to spoil all the events so far, with the help of his sneaky goblin servants.

Jack Frost knew that the Showtime
Fairies' magic stars had the power to
bring out everyone's talents to their best
abilities, and had stolen the stars from
the ends of their wands while they'd
been rehearsing for the Fairyland talent
show. Then he'd sent his goblins to the
human world with the magic stars to
wreck the student auditions.

The goblins, however,
hadn't been able
to resist entering
the auditions
themselves,
pretending to be
from a school called
Icy Towers. The magic
stars were so powerful that they'd
made the goblins seem extra talented!

13

Luckily, Kirsty, Rachel and the Showtime Fairies had managed to get the magic stars back and prevent the goblins from winning each time. But now Jack Frost had found out about this, and had vowed to come to tonight's Variety Show and spoil it himself!

"We've got to find Taylor the Talent Show Fairy's missing star," Kirsty whispered to Rachel. "If we can't get it back to her before the show starts, the whole thing could be a disaster anyway, whether Jack Frost turns up or not!"

Rachel agreed. While the other six Showtime Fairies looked after individual talents such as dancing and singing, Taylor's star ensured that when different talents came together in a contest, everything would run smoothly.

14

"Fingers crossed," Rachel said. "We've still got some time before the show begins. And anything can happen when fairies are involved!"

"I-i-i-t's showtime!" said Mr Walker in a loud voice just then, making both girls jump. They burst out laughing when they saw him wearing a blue and gold sparkly wig. He grinned. "Well, I've got to support Tippington School, haven't I?" he said. "There's a stall over there selling souvenirs. I couldn't resist."

He gave each of the girls some money. "Why don't you have a look? They've got wigs, flags, all sorts of things."

"Thanks, Dad," Rachel said. She arranged to meet her parents after the show, then headed towards the stall with Kirsty. There was a crowd of children and parents buying souvenirs, and Kirsty and Rachel had to queue for a few minutes to buy Tippington badges and flags.

As she paid for her flag, Kirsty couldn't help noticing that it seemed brighter than all the others. *Is one of the spotlights shining on it?* she wondered. Then she unfurled the flag...and blinked in delight when she saw what – or rather *who* – fluttered out. Taylor the Talent Show Fairy!

Curtain Up

Kirsty and Rachel had met all seven Showtime Fairies at the start of the week and were pleased to see the pretty blonde fairy again now. Taylor wore a lilac flower-patterned dress and gold wedge-heeled shoes with ribbon ties. Golden bangles sparkled on one wrist, and she had a matching star pendant.

"Hello!" Kirsty whispered. "Quick, hide in my pocket before anyone sees you!"

Taylor fluttered her gauzy wings and made a dive for Kirsty's pocket. And just in time, too! Before the girls could catch their breath from the excitement of seeing Taylor, two of Rachel's school friends, Josie and Maya, came up to say hello.

"Hi, guys!" smiled Josie.

Rachel's heart was thumping. Thank goodness Josie and Maya hadn't appeared two seconds earlier! "Hi," she said. "I can't wait for the show to begin."

"Me too!"
Maya said.
"There's
something
strange
going on,
though. Do
you remember
that team from Icy

Towers at our audition – the boys who
made everyone laugh with their funny
acrobatics? Well, they're not here – and
nor is anybody else from that school."

Kirsty felt her face turn hot, despite the
cool evening air. Icy Towers wasn't a
real school, of course – the goblins had
made it up so that they could take part
in the auditions. But she couldn't tell
Josie and Maya that!

A huge roar went up from the audience just then and all four girls swung round to see two people walking on stage. "Quick!" Josie cried. "There's Andy and Jess. The show's starting!"

Josie and Maya hurried off to sit near Josie's parents, and Rachel and Kirsty rushed to find some spare seats nearby, at the end of a row. Andy and Jess were two television presenters who were hosting the talent show, and now they stood in front of the closed stage curtain.

Taylor popped her head out of Kirsty's pocket. "I'm getting a strong feeling my star is around here somewhere," she said in a tinkling voice. "But I'm not quite sure where…"

"Hello, everyone, and welcome!" said Andy, to thunderous applause.

"We're delighted to be here at Cooke Stadium tonight," said Jess. "We've got a fantastic line-up, starting with—" She broke off in surprise as the stage curtain rose behind her...and an icy chill went around the stadium.

Rachel and Kirsty nearly fell off their seats when they saw who was standing behind the curtain in a sparkly ice-blue cloak. Jack Frost!

"Oh no!" Rachel gasped.

Jack Frost sneered out at the audience with cold eyes that glittered with malice. People in the audience began to shiver, and a thin layer of sparkling white frost formed on the stage around him.

"Oh!" Andy exclaimed, exchanging a confused glance with Jess. She shrugged, also looking baffled.

"Well, we knew it was going to be a show of surprises, but this mysterious man in the blue cloak has surprised even us!"

The audience laughed, still shivering. They obviously thought that Jack Frost was part of the evening's entertainment – when, of course, all he wanted to do was spoil things.

Taylor quickly waved her wand, sending shimmering golden fairy magic straight at the curtain. This made it lower once more, hiding Jack Frost.

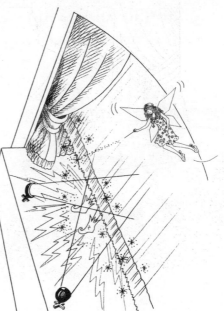

"We've got to stop him!" Taylor whispered. "Girls, I'll turn you into fairies. Let's go behind the souvenir stall so nobody can see us!"

Rachel and Kirsty ducked behind the stall, and Taylor sprinkled some fairy dust over them, making them shrink to fairy-size. Now they had their very own glittering fairy wings, and could zoom into the air, just like Taylor.

"Let's head for the stage," Rachel said, soaring up high so nobody would see her. "Come on!"

Hiding in the shadows, way above the stadium, the three fairies whizzed towards the backstage area.

Jack Frost was pulling angrily at the curtain and trying to open it again. Luckily, Taylor's magic held strong, making it impossible.

"Useless thing!" he fumed, pointing a finger at one of the stage lights. An icy bolt shot from his fingertip, smashing the light and turning it dark. "Ha!" he laughed bitterly. "I'm going to enjoy ruining this stupid show. I'll make everyone wish they'd stayed at home!"

Ice Fire

"That's what *you* think!" Taylor blurted out, swooping daringly towards Jack Frost. She put her hands on her hips and glared at him. "Give us that star back right now!"

Jack Frost gave a horrible laugh, as if that was the very last thing he planned to do. Then he pointed a bony finger at Taylor, sending an ice bolt hurtling

towards her. With
a squeal of fright, she
dodged out of the
way, and Jack Frost
laughed all the
harder. "Pathetic!"
he jeered.

"Come on,
Rachel,"
Kirsty
murmured.
"Let's
look for
where he's
hidden the
star. It must be
somewhere nearby."

Kirsty, Rachel and Taylor flew around
Jack Frost, hoping to spot Taylor's star.

Jack Frost swatted at them, as if they were annoying flies. "Buzz off," he grumbled. "Go on, shoo! Can't you see I'm busy? I've got a talent show to wreck!"

"Not if we can help it!" Rachel panted, ducking quickly as Jack Frost sent another icy blast at her.

"I'm afraid we're just having a few technical problems," the girls and Taylor heard Jess say to the audience, as the ice bolts banged and crashed behind the curtain. "I'm sure everything will be fixed soon."

Meanwhile, Jack Frost was blasting ice bolts at the fairies from every direction. Each time, they nimbly swerved and swooped, avoiding the icy missiles, but Kirsty was starting to feel tired.

How much longer could they keep this up? And where was Taylor's magic star? Maybe Jack Frost had hidden it somewhere in Fairyland, and didn't even have it with him any longer!

CRASH! One of Jack Frost's ice bolts slammed into a machine at the side of the stage, and a wisp of white smoke curled out of it. "The dry ice machine!" Taylor cried in alarm, as smoke began gushing out. "Uh-oh. Let me see if I can fix that…"

While Taylor worked her magic on
the dry ice machine, Jack Frost took
aim at her.

"Leave her alone!" Rachel yelled,
zooming past his face to distract him.

Startled, Jack Frost batted at her,
sending his ice bolt crashing up towards
the stage curtain instead of at Taylor.
There was a whirring sound,
and the curtain began rising.

"Oh no!" Taylor cried,
spinning round from the
mended dry ice machine.
"He's broken the curtain
mechanism – and
broken the spell
I cast. Quick – fly
up high before the
audience sees us!"

Rachel and Kirsty shot into the air after Taylor and hid in the shadowy lighting rig, out of sight. Now the curtain was all the way up, and Jack Frost was visible for everyone to see.

"Oh dear," Jess was saying, with a puzzled frown. "I do apologise, ladies and gentlemen, I'm not quite sure what—"

Her voice trailed away as Jack Frost hopped around, swatting his hands through the air.

"Where are those fairies? *Where are
those fairies?*" he bellowed furiously,
hopping up and down.

Then he caught sight of Taylor's
shimmering wings poking out behind
one of the lights. He leapt up, trying
to snatch at her. "I see you! I see you
hiding from me!"

Someone in the audience giggled.

"OK…" Andy said slowly, pulling a
funny face at the audience. "Fairies, eh?"

Meanwhile, the curtain was closing
again, cutting Jack Frost off from the
stage. As soon as it was fully down,
the three fairies flew towards Jack Frost,
trying to spot the star.

But it was no good – the curtain was
opening again, and they had to zoom
back to their hiding place!

35

The curtain carried on opening and closing. By now, the audience were laughing hysterically whenever it rose to reveal Jack Frost thrashing around, still trying to swipe the fairies. "They think this is a comedy routine," Taylor giggled, and Kirsty and Rachel couldn't help chuckling too. Jack Frost might be horribly scary and bad-tempered, but he did look funny, hopping around wildly on stage as if he had ants in his pants!

Just then, Rachel spotted rainbow colours shimmering underneath Jack Frost's cold white beard.

"It's your star, Taylor, look!" she gasped. "It's attached to the top of his cape, like a clasp."

Kirsty's face fell. "How on earth are we going to get *that*?" she whispered.

Taylor bit her lip as they watched Jack Frost scowling at the audience. He looked angrier than ever.

"You'll be sorry you laughed at me," he spat, and raised a finger, as if he were going to fire one of his ice bolts right into the front row.

"Oh no!" Taylor cried. "We've got to stop him. Right now!"

Escape to Fairyland

Taylor waved her wand just in time, and a stream of sparkling golden fairy magic poured from its tip, knocking Jack Frost's ice bolt off course, and causing it to bounce harmlessly down on the stage. "I've got to get him away from here," she said. "If I could just magic him to Fairyland without anyone seeing…"

"I know!" Rachel cried, swooping down to the dry ice machine. She found a switch marked "On", and leant against it as hard as she could. The switch clicked on…then out billowed a thick cloud of dry ice, blanketing the entire stage with white smoke!

"Perfect!" Kirsty laughed, and Taylor immediately waved her wand, sending sparkles flying around the three friends and Jack Frost. A glittering whirlwind appeared, lifting them up and whisking them away at top speed.

"Stop!" Jack Frost howled, his voice muffled by the whirlwind. "I haven't finished ruining the talent show yet!"

"Oh yes, you have," Taylor muttered.

Seconds later they landed, and the whirlwind cleared to reveal that they were standing in a beautiful glade in Fairyland, full of flowering shrubs.
And there were the other six Showtime Fairies — Madison, Leah, Alesha, Darcey, Amelia and Isla, who rushed over in delight.

"You've got your magic star back, hooray!" beamed Alesha.

"We were about to start rehearsing for tonight's show — you're just in time!" smiled Isla.

They hadn't spotted Jack Frost, who was standing with his back to them. Now he turned, glaring.

"She *hasn't* got the magic star back, actually," he said coldly. Then he noticed that the fairies had props with them, to use in their rehearsal, and a horrible smile appeared on his face. "You might have stopped  me ruining the humans' talent show, but I've just had an even better idea. I'll ruin your stupid *fairy* show instead!"

He rushed at Madison, knocking her top hat off, flung Alesha's acrobat ribbons into a puddle, and tossed Darcey's ballet shoes up into a tree.

"Oh no!" Kirsty gasped, but the fairies merely shrugged.

"Don't worry," Leah said, as he trampled over her costumes. "We can magic everything to rights when he's calmed down. The most important thing is that we get Taylor's star back as soon as possible, otherwise tonight's show could be awful!"

"The star is fastened to his cape, hidden under his beard," Rachel told the others.

"And I've had an idea how we can get it!" Kirsty added. "If he wants a terrible talent show, let's give him one!" She explained her plan in whispers and the fairies grinned in delight.

"Brilliant," Taylor giggled. Then she said in a louder voice, so that Jack Frost could hear, "Well, we're going to have to rehearse even though we haven't got my magic star back. The show must go on! I just hope we can make it a *good* show…"

With a few knowing looks and stifled giggles, the Showtime Fairies pretended to practise their acts, helped by Kirsty and Rachel. But instead of trying to perform at their best, the fairies deliberately made their performances far worse than usual. Amelia burst into song, only her voice was off-key, and she had a huge fake coughing fit in the middle. Madison pulled a bunch of carrots from her hat, and stared at them in dismay.

"Oh dear!" she groaned. "I've got my rabbit-in-the-hat trick wrong *again*!"

Jack Frost was watching the fairies from a short distance away. His mouth twitched with amusement as Darcey stumbled over a tree root during a too-fast pirouette and bumped into Isla, who was trying, and failing, to skate across the grass.

47

Then he sniggered as Leah's wig slipped over her eyes during her dramatic speech. "Hey, who turned out the lights?" she cried.

Jack Frost laughed out loud when Kirsty pretended she was practising a handstand but had forgotten to put her legs in the air, and when Rachel started telling a joke and got the wrong punchline.

And then,
as Alesha did
an acrobatic
routine
that ended
with her
backflipping
straight into
the lake,
Jack Frost
burst into fits
of laughter. He
was laughing so
hard, he didn't notice
the fairies exchanging glances.

"Now!" hissed Kirsty.

A Tutu Trap!

Alesha clambered quickly out of the
lake, then she and Taylor stretched one
of her acrobat ribbons across the glade,
just near Jack Frost's legs. Kirsty and
Rachel, meanwhile, had grabbed one
of Darcey's tutu skirts and were holding
it at the ready.

Jack Frost, still chortling, stumbled into
the low ribbon, tripped and fell…straight
through the open tutu

skirt, pinning his arms
to his body!

"Hey!" he yelled
crossly, trying to
wriggle free.

Her heart pounding,
Kirsty lifted his icy
beard and grabbed the
magic star, then threw
it to Taylor. Immediately,
the star shrank to its usual size and
Taylor was able to slot it back on the
end of her wand, where it belonged.

"Oh…*bother!*" Jack Frost snarled,
glowering at Kirsty and Rachel. "Now
you've spoiled all my fun!"

The girls carefully helped him out of the tutu. "I don't think you need that star anyway," Rachel said, slightly nervous at being so near Jack Frost when he was in such a bad temper. "You were brilliant on stage back in the Cooke Stadium. The audience loved you!"

"Hmmph," muttered Jack Frost sulkily, but Kirsty noticed that he wasn't scowling quite so much any more.

"She's right," Kirsty said quickly. "I think you're a natural comedian.

And so many people get stage fright about performing in front of an audience, but you didn't. Who needs a star, with your confidence and talent?"

The tutu came off, and Jack Frost was released. Kirsty and Rachel stepped back, worried he might unleash more icy blasts at them, but he seemed thoughtful.

"A natural comedian, eh?" he repeated, as if trying on the words for size. "Confidence and talent?"

"Absolutely," said Taylor, joining the conversation. "In fact, you're just what our talent show needs: a bit of comedy. Why don't you and your goblins see if you can put a routine together for tonight?"

Jack Frost looked pleased. "That's not a bad idea," he said. "After all, making

54

people laugh does take real talent."

"Oh, definitely," Taylor agreed. "One
of the best talents to have, I'd say."

Jack Frost's icy face seemed to be on
the verge of cracking a smile. "Well…
maybe," he said gruffly. "If you're
lucky." And he stalked off hurriedly, as if
secretly he couldn't wait to get started.

That afternoon in Fairyland, the audience gathered to watch the talent show, with King Oberon and Queen Titania sitting in the front row. Kirsty and Rachel had been asked to introduce the acts

and they both felt tingly with excitement as they walked on stage. They were so lucky to be able to visit Fairyland and have adventures with the fairies!

"Hello, everyone," Kirsty said, smiling as she recognised many fairy friends in the audience. "We're really thrilled to be here at the Fairyland Talent Show."

"Our first act is a dance routine, put together by Darcey the Dance Diva Fairy, starring Darcey and the Dance Fairies!" said Rachel.

The audience clapped, and Rachel and Kirsty went to the side of the stage. The background music began, and out came Darcey, followed by six of the Dance Fairies: Bethany, Jade, Rebecca, Tasha, Jessica and Saskia.

Their routine included many different dance styles and costumes, from ballet to tap to salsa, with some disco moves thrown in for good measure, too.

Then came Amelia who sang amazingly to a beautiful piece of music played by the seven Music Fairies. She was followed by Alesha the Acrobat Fairy and Gemma the Gymnastics Fairy, who put on a breathtaking performance together.

Madison's magic show made the audience *ooh* and *ahh* as she pulled not one, not two, but *three* white rabbits from her top hat. Leah starred in an exciting play alongside some  of her fairy friends, and then Jack Frost helpfully turned the stage to ice so that Isla the Ice Star Fairy and Imogen the Ice Dance Fairy could demonstrate their incredible ice-skating skills.

The audience clapped and cheered, then Queen Titania used her magic to remove the ice. Kirsty and Rachel walked back on stage to introduce the last act of the evening.

"We hope you've enjoyed the show so far," Rachel said. "We certainly have!"

"For our final act, we've got something rather special," Kirsty said. "Prepare to laugh your socks off…it's Jack Frost and the Goblin Gang!"

The girls withdrew to the side of the stage, their fingers crossed. They hoped this would work!

A Fabulous Finale

A murmur of surprise went around the audience as Jack Frost and the goblins walked on stage. Jack Frost was known throughout Fairyland for his unkind tricks and spiteful ways. What was he doing here?

"I say, I say, I say," Jack Frost began. He cleared his throat nervously. "What do you call a..." Then he seemed lost for words, as if he'd forgotten the rest of the joke. He waved a hand agitatedly... accidentally causing a blast of icy magic to shoot across the stage, turning it into a freezing cold ice slide!

Seeing this, one of the goblins mischievously pushed another, sending him skidding along the ice.

"Wheeeee!" the second goblin squealed, holding his arms out like a surfer. "Hey, this is cool!" The other goblins tried out the ice slide, seeming to forget about the routine, and the audience laughed as they toppled into one another, fell over and skidded about. Nobody was hurt – in fact, the goblins were having a whale of a time, which made the whole thing even funnier.

65

Jack Frost had a go on the ice slide himself, remembering his jokes and shouting them at the top of his voice while he did so. Soon the audience were almost crying with laughter at the spectacle. "I never knew he could be so funny!" Queen Titania chuckled, dabbing at her eyes. "He's hilarious!"

"The best comedy routine I've ever seen," King Oberon agreed, guffawing as a goblin skidded around on one leg, accidentally kicking another goblin over.

Rachel and Kirsty were breathless with giggles, too. Then, when the act was finally over, the audience rose to their feet, clapping harder than ever. The goblins and Jack Frost bowed, clearly delighted with the applause and cheers. The act had been a huge success — everyone had loved it!

Queen Titania used her magic once more to clear away the ice, then she and King Oberon walked onto the stage.

"Well! What a wonderful evening,"
she said, smiling broadly. "We'd like to
invite all our performers back on stage so
that we can give them one last round of
applause."

On came the Showtime Fairies again,
with Jack Frost, the goblins and all the
other fairies who'd taken part. The
audience clapped and cheered as they
took their bows.

"Wait," King Oberon said. "Not
everyone is here. Kirsty and Rachel –
you need to be on stage, too!"

Kirsty and Rachel looked at one
another in surprise.

"But Your Majesty, we didn't do
anything in the talent show," Rachel
said, feeling rather awkward as she and
Kirsty joined the performers.

68

Queen Titania smiled. "Everyone has a talent," she said, "and yours is very special indeed. Being talented isn't just about performing for an audience. Your special talent is that you are so friendly and helpful – and you've always been very brave, whenever you've helped us. I think I speak for all the fairies when I say that we're extremely grateful to you for that."

"Hear, hear," King Oberon agreed. "A round of applause for Kirsty and Rachel!"

Rachel and Kirsty felt goosebumps as the audience rose to their feet and clapped harder than they'd done all night. Being friends with the fairies was so wonderful!

"And now I'm afraid it's time to send you back to your own world," Queen Titania said. "Thanks again. Enjoy the rest of the show!"

She waved her wand, casting a golden sparkling whirlwind around Kirsty and Rachel, which took them spinning away from Fairyland. *Enjoy the rest of the show?* Kirsty thought in confusion. But the fairies' show had finished!

She blinked as she and Rachel landed behind the souvenir stall again. Of course! She'd had such an amazing time in Fairyland, she'd quite forgotten about the talent show taking place in the human world.

"Let's sit down and watch," she said. "We've only been away for a few seconds. Come on!"

On stage, Andy and Jess were fanning away the dry ice. Then, as it cleared, Andy stared in surprise at the empty stage. "Oh! Our mysterious friend has vanished. Let's get started without any further ado."

"There's just time to tell you that tonight's show has raised a huge amount of money," Jess said. "As you know, we're raising funds to refurbish Oval Park, and I'm delighted to say that enough money has come in to buy a new adventure playground, a bandstand *and* an outdoor theatre."

"That's not all," Andy added with a smile. "With the extra money raised, there's going to be a new fairy grotto, too!"

Kirsty and Rachel smiled at each other. They hoped some of their fairy friends would come and visit it!

"Now for our first act, who wowed the judges at the magic show auditions,"

Jess continued. "Please give a big hand to our wonderful junior magician. It's Holly!"

Everyone clapped as Rachel's friend Holly came on stage, and Rachel and Kirsty settled back in their seats, all set to enjoy the show. With Taylor's magic star back in place, they knew that everything would go perfectly. All in all, it had been another marvellously magical half-term holiday!

Now it's time for Kirsty and Rachel to help...

Selena the Sleepover Fairy

Read on for a sneak peek...

"I feel as if it's my birthday and Christmas at the same time!" said Rachel Walker, bouncing up and down on her coach seat. "I can't believe we're actually going to a sleepover in the National Museum!"

"It makes it twice as exciting that you're here," agreed her best friend, Kirsty Tate, sitting down beside her. "It was so kind of the headmaster to let you come along."

Kirsty's school had won a place in a giant eco-charity sleepover, which was being held at the National Museum. Thirty children from the school were going to the city to take part. Rachel was staying with Kirsty, and so she had been allowed to join in, too.

The coach driver took his place and the engine rumbled into life. As the coach drew out of the school car park, the girls waved goodbye to Kirsty's mum, who had come to see them off.

"I hope it's not spooky there at night," said a girl called Hannah, who was sitting in the seat behind Rachel. "I'm a bit scared of the dark..."

Read Selena the Sleepover Fairy
to find out what adventures are in store for
Kirsty and Rachel!

Meet the
Showtime Fairies

Meet the fairies, play games
and get sneak peeks at
the latest books!

www.rainbowmagicbooks.co.uk

There's fairy fun for everyone at
www.rainbowmagicbooks.co.uk.
You'll find great activities, competitions, stories and
fairy profiles, and also a special newsletter.

Competition!

If you study these four pictures of Madison the Magic Show Fairy very carefully you'll see that one of them is slightly different from the others. Can you work out which one is the odd one out? Make a note of the name of this book and the letter and when you have enjoyed all seven books in the Showtime Fairies series, send the answers in to us!

A

B

C

D

We will put all of the correct entries into a draw and
select one winner to receive a special **Rainbow Magic
Showtime Fairies Pack** featuring lots of treats!

Enter online now at

www.rainbowmagicbooks.co.uk

No purchase required. Only one entry per child. Two prize
draws will take place on 29 July 2011 and 28 October 2011.
Alternatively, readers can send the seven answers on a postcard to:
Rainbow Magic Showtime Fairies Competition, Orchard Books,
338 Euston Road, London NW1 3BH. Australian readers can write to:
Rainbow Magic Showtime Fairies Competition, Hachette Children's Books,
level 17/207 Kent St, Sydney, NSW 2000.
E-mail: childrens.books@hachette.com.au

Meet the
Princess Fairies

Out in Aug

Out in Oct

Jack Frost has stolen the Princess Fairies' tiaras. Kirsty and Rachel must get them back before all the magic in the world fades away!

www.rainbowmagicbooks.co.uk